A Note from the Author

The idea for this story came to me because I like food so much. I'm lucky, I don't put on much weight because I'm always rushing around. But last year we went on holiday in Greece. The food was wonderful. I swam a lot, I walked a lot, but I ate a REAL lot. When I got home I knew something had to be done! I cut out bread and potatoes, pizza and pasta, and only ate things that were really good for me. This plan didn't work very well. My son told me I was *still* eating too much. Broccoli is good for you, roast chicken is good for you. Salad is very good for you. But you have to leave out the mayo, and the melted butter, or you will never get slim – and I hadn't planned for that.

My idea was that *someone*, somewhere, must be able to help me with my weakness for delicious food, and that's what made me think of "The Visitor". But as Tom finds out, when someone comes along and offers to grant your dearest wish, there's often a catch.

The Visitor

by

Ann Halam

First published in 2006 in Great Britain by
Barrington Stoke Ltd
www.barringtonstoke.co.uk

ISBN-10: 1-84299-416-0
ISBN-13: 978-1-84299-416-0

Printed in Great Britain by Bell & Bain Ltd

Contents

Chapter 1
Experiment House

Tom woke up early on the first day of his work experience. He was going to work with his dad for two weeks. He had to eat some chocolate biscuits before he even got up because he was feeling so tense and excited. His dad was the head security guard at Experiment House. Tom could see Experiment House from his bedroom window. He could see tall fences, and the dark trees all round it.

Experiment House was the big house on a hill at the edge of town. No one, not even Tom's dad, knew what went on in the labs there. Scientists worked for the government there. Dad said it was Top Secret.

Tom liked the idea of being a security guard. He liked the idea of the uniform. As he ate his biscuits, he thought about going on patrol with a big guard dog on a choke chain and flashlight. He was so thrilled, he thought about that more than the biscuits he was eating. He forgot to enjoy them. They were his favourite sort, with creamy toffee inside and chocolate on the outside. But when the packet was empty, Tom didn't even remember what they had tasted like. He licked around his mouth and looked on the pillow for crumbs. Just as he was feeling sad and a bit fed up that he hadn't enjoyed them more, the smell of his mum's best crispy bacon drifted up the stairs. Tom cheered up.

In the kitchen, his dad and his sister Molly were grabbing their breakfasts while they got ready for work. Tom sat down and focused on his bacon and eggs and baked beans. He thought you should always respect nice food. You shouldn't just gobble it up.

"Are you sure I'm going to have a uniform, Dad?" he asked.

"I'm sure," said Dad. "I asked Mrs Stevens. She's in charge of uniforms. She wanted to know how tall you are."

"Did you tell her how *fat* he is?" asked Molly.

"Leave him alone," said Tom's mum. "It's puppy fat. He'll grow out of it."

Tom looked back at his dad. Dad went running every morning. He was skinny as a string bean. Molly was thin too. She ate what she liked and never put on weight. Tom's mum loved cooking, but she never ate too much. Tom was the fat one of the family. It didn't seem fair, but what could he do? He *loved* food! He'd tried jogging, but he hated it.

He glared at Molly, then took a big mouthful of bacon and beans.

"Can we take the camera to work?" he asked, when he could speak.

He wanted a photo of himself in security guard uniform, to show the kids at school. It's not easy being fat and fifteen. At last, he would be able to impress people.

"No cameras allowed," said Dad. "We'll ask Mrs Stevens if you can bring your uniform home one night."

"How would *you* catch someone trying to break in?" Molly said with a grin. "Sit on him?"

"You're just jealous," said Tom. "*You* only work at the stupid dentist's. Dad? Will I be taught how to handle the dogs? Will I have a weapon?"

"We'll see," said Tom's dad. "Get a move on, Tom. We don't want to be late."

"One more piece of toast," said Tom, firmly.

He always finished breakfast with one slice of toast and jam, and one slice of toast and marmite. If he ate them too fast, the tastes of jam and marmite got mixed up. In the end, he had to take his marmite toast to the car with him.

He licked marmite from around his mouth as they drove through the check-point at the gates of Experiment House. The guard gave Dad a salute. Tom gave the guard a salute back, and then hoped that wasn't baby-ish. But the guard grinned. Soon Tom would be wearing that same smart uniform. It was the greatest day of his life.

His best friend Richie was working with his mother at the hospital flower shop. Everyone had laughed at him, and said it was a girly job. *Poor Richie!* thought Tom. *He may be thin, but I'm the one who's got lucky. My work experience is going to be the best.*

****

At the front desk Tom had his fingerprints taken. A weird camera eye on the desk took his photo. He wished he could have had the photo taken when he had his uniform. The guards at the front desk let him come round and look at their CCTV screens. All you could see were empty corridors, but Tom was thrilled. Then a tall man in a white coat, with frizzy brown hair, came down the stairs and walked up to the front desk.

"Hello, Dan," he said. Dan was Tom's dad's name. "So this is young Tom?"

"Yes, sir."

"I'm Dr Wilson," said the man in the white coat. "I'm Chief Science Officer here. Glad to have you with us, young man." He shook Tom's hand.

Tom flushed with pride. Dr Wilson was the top boss. Dr Wilson said a few more friendly things then he headed for some swing doors where there was a sign which said **No Public Beyond This Point**. A light flashed as he pushed open the door. Even the boss had to be checked every time he went into the labs. *Soon they'll let me in there*, thought Tom.

"Right, Tom," said Tom's dad. "Time we got you your uniform."

Dad took Tom to the supply room. They didn't have to go through a security check to get there. The supply room was next to the canteen, and that part of Experiment House wasn't Top Secret. Dad always took in sandwiches for his lunch, and he'd made some for Tom, but Tom sniffed at the cooking smells in the canteen. Sometimes at school there were very good hot dinners. Tom thought he'd eat his sandwiches if he had a morning break. *Then for lunch I might have shepherd's pie*, he thought. *Crispy on top, with real Heinz ketchup.*

Or sausages and mash, with onion gravy ...

When she saw Tom, Mrs Stevens the Supplies Manager shook her head. "Oh, dear," she said. "Dan, you only told me his height. You didn't tell me he was, um, so *plump*!" She looked in a locker, where security guard uniforms, white coats and overalls were folded on shelves, and brought out one for Tom to try.

He took it into the changing room. It was very smart, but he couldn't do up the buttons on the jacket. Mrs Stevens picked another, and he couldn't zip up the trousers. Then she took out an *enormous* uniform. Tom could do it up, but the sleeves hung down to his knees and the bottoms of the trousers fell all round his feet.

By this time Tom was bright red in the face. He wanted to die.

"He can wear his own clothes," said Tom's dad. "It doesn't matter."

"I can't allow that," said Mrs Stevens. She had taken Tom's own clothes and put them in a locker, except for his underwear and his shoes and socks. "This is a government lab. He has to be properly dressed. He can have a Clean-Suit. They fit *anyone*."

The Clean-Suit was like big crinkly pale green baby-pyjamas. It had a hood you could pull over your head, and bootees that went over your shoes. Mrs Stevens had to help Tom to put it on.

He was so embarrassed, he just let it happen.

"It's what the scientists wear in the top security labs," said Tom's dad, trying to cheer him up. "When they're doing something risky. It's for important work –"

Tom looked at himself in the mirror, and saw a huge, giant green baby.

"That's OK," he croaked. "But what can I wear to go on patrol?"

"Well, that's something I have to explain," said Tom's dad. "Come on, chum. I'll show you where you're going to work this morning."

He took Tom to a little room full of tall steel cabinets. It was along the same corridor as the supply room. There was a big stack of papers in a basket on the desk.

"Don't worry about Shirley Stevens," said Dad. "She's sometimes rude to people."

Tom shook his head. He didn't want to talk about it.

"You'll be working in here," Dad went on. "Someone needs to file all those papers in the right order, A to Z. It's important."

"OK," said Tom. "But will I be going on patrol with you, as well?"

"Er, no," said Dad, looking away from Tom. "The truth is, Tom, you'll be in here all the time. Dr Wilson let you come to Experiment House for your work experience as a big favour. You can't really work with the security guards. I'm sorry, I know you thought you were going to."

"But I had my photo taken and my fingerprints done and everything!"

"That was so you'd know what it's like," Dad said. "You must understand, Tom. This is a Top Secret place, and this is just your work experience."

Tom suddenly knew that he didn't want anyone to see him in the green baby-suit anyway. "You should have told me all that before," he said.

"I didn't want to show you up in front of Molly," said Dad. "She teases you enough already. Look, no one need know. You'll still be able to tell them at school that you were a security guard. And I'll take you to see the dogs in their kennel."

"Thanks very much," said Tom, but he couldn't sound grateful.

"This filing is *important* work," said Tom's dad. He sounded very unhappy.

"Leave me alone, Dad," said Tom.

Tom was too proud to show how upset he was. Dad had been feeling sorry for him. That was why he'd got Tom this stupid pretend work experience job. Tom sat down at the desk.

"I'll get on with it," he said. "I'm OK."

Chapter 2

Food Can Ruin Your Life

Tom tried to take the horrible baby-suit off, but he remembered he was only wearing his vest and pants under it, so he gave up. He did some filing, to make the time go by. It was easy. The papers all had titles at the top. All he had to do was put papers with names that started with 'A' in a folder marked 'A', and so on until he got to 'Z'.

At 10.30 he ate his tuna sandwiches and drank his juice. At eleven o' clock he ate the rest of his lunch – a piece of home-made apple-pie and a banana. When all the food

was gone he felt as if he'd lost his only friends in the world. There were more papers to sort, but he was sick of it. He was so bored, he fell asleep with his head on the desk.

He woke up suddenly. The clock on the wall said one o'clock, and his stomach was telling him it was lunchtime. He thought he would check out the canteen. Maybe other people would be wearing Clean-Suits, so he wouldn't feel stupid. Then he remembered, Alison was coming to see him.

She would be waiting for him now, outside the car park!

Alison was Tom's girlfriend. She was really pretty and very kind and gentle. She had been his girlfriend since Easter. They had met at a party, and started talking, and got to like each other. Tom still couldn't believe his luck.

He'd promised her that his Dad would show her around! Oh, no!

He ran out of the filing room, down the corridor to the front hall and right past the front desk. No one stopped him. He was in such a hurry he'd forgotten about the Clean-Suit. He had to stop at the checkpoint gates. He was all puffed out. *Then* he remembered the Clean-Suit. The guard on duty was grinning. Even the dogs seemed to be trying not to laugh. Tom could see Alison. She was standing under a tree by the road, staring at him. She looked at him in horror.

"Hello, Tom," she said, as he came up. "Er, what's that you've got on? What happened to your security guard uniform?"

"This is a Clean-Suit," said Tom. He tried to make it sound cool. "It's what we have to wear in the labs. It's a special sort of overall for the labs. To protect us."

"Oh, Tom," said Alison. "You look like the Green Blob from Outer Space."

First she laughed, and then suddenly she began to cry. She sat down on the grass by the road, and hid her face in her hands. Tom didn't know what to do. She kept on crying, so he sat down beside her and tried to put his arm round her. He was glad there was no one watching them.

Alison jerked away from him, and started crying harder.

"I'll have a uniform tomorrow," Tom lied. "They're getting one ready for me."

"Tom," sobbed Alison, "I can't go on with this."

"With what?" asked Tom.

He knew something terrible was about to happen.

"I said I'd go out with you because I felt sorry for you, at that party," cried Alison. "And then all this time I didn't know how to say I wanted to break up –"

She still had her hands over her face. He thought she could at least look at him, while she was telling him she'd been lying for months –

"What have I done wrong?" yelled Tom. He was hurt, but he was very angry too. "I know this green pyjama-suit looks funny. You can't judge me by the clothes I have to wear at work! That's horrible. That's so shallow!"

"It's not the suit."

Alison looked up. When he saw the look on her face he knew she would never be nice to him again. "All right, I'll say it. It's because you're *fat*, Tom. And you deserve to be fat. All you think about is food, food, food! Call me what you like. You're gross. I'm embarrassed to be seen around with you ... because you're *so fat!*"

She jumped up and ran away. She didn't look back.

Tom felt terrible. He knew he'd never get another girlfriend. What was worse, he knew Alison had never really been kind. She'd only been too much of a coward to tell the truth. And now they weren't going out, she'd tell all her friends about the stupid green baby-suit.

Tom had been tough about not going on patrol, and about the baby-suit. Breaking up with Alison, on top of everything else, was too much. The rest of the day passed by in a fog. He was too desperate to care about anything. He changed back into his own clothes feeling like a beaten dog. At home, when they all sat down to dinner, he couldn't stop himself from crying.

"I hate my life," he sobbed. "I can't stand being so fat!"

"Come running with me," said Dad. "You'll soon lose those kilos."

Mum came round to his chair, and gave him a hug. "We'll all help,' she said. "I'll make you special meals. You can have salads. Roast chicken, eggs, fish. No more bread, pasta or potatoes. No more sugary treats. That'll do the trick."

"I'll help you too," said Molly with a grin. "I'll start now."

She took Tom's dinner from under his nose, and shifted one of his lamb chops and most of the delicious new potatoes onto her own plate.

Mum and Dad yelled at Molly – for teasing Tom when he was so down.

But Tom's plate was still pretty full, and he still wanted to eat the lot. Mum's grilled lamb chops with garlic were so delicious, and

Tom *loved* fresh new potatoes in their skins, with lots of melted butter.

He felt let down. Mum and Dad were just like Alison. They'd *pretended* they didn't mind that he was fat. The truth was they had no respect for him. Tom knew that running wasn't the answer. He would lose weight, and then stop running, and then get fat again. He would have to go running every day *forever*, and he couldn't stand the idea. Special meals wouldn't work either. He would just eat *more* of the healthy food. He loved salad. He loved roast chicken.

"You don't understand," he said. "Nobody understands. I'm going to bed."

****

Tom went to his room and sat on his bed. He noticed how it sagged as he sat down. He hated being fat, but tonight he was so

21

unhappy he felt he needed a treat. He looked under the bed for his biscuits. Then he remembered that he'd eaten them all. *OK, I won't eat anything until breakfast*, he decided.

This is the start of a new me.

He woke around midnight. He felt so hungry. The fridge seemed to be humming to him, *Come on Tom, come to me ...* Half-asleep, he made his way downstairs in the dark and opened the fridge door. The beautiful light inside shone on one of Mum's syrup tarts. No one had eaten any of it. Next to the golden, chewy tart there was a jug of thick, smooth cream.

Tom took them both upstairs.

It's Mum's fault, he thought, and ate a sweet, gooey slice.

Why does she have to cook so well? Why does she have to leave syrup tart in the fridge?

It's Dad's fault.

He should stop me. He should punish me for eating too much.

By the third slice all his excuses were gone, and he didn't care.

It's no use, Tom told himself. *I just* love *food. Food is my best friend.*

He hadn't switched on his light. He liked to be in the dark when he was having a midnight feast. Through his window he could see Experiment House. Something was going on up there. He could see flashlights bobbing among the spooky trees. A stream of black jeeps with huge headlights zoomed out of the car park. *Maybe there's been a disaster*, he thought. He was glad Dad wasn't on night shift.

Just for a moment he thought about how it would be if he was out there with the other guards. He'd be in his uniform and he'd be the bravest of them all.

Then all the horrific things that had really happened to him at Experiment House rushed back into his mind. Tom lay down and pulled the covers over his head.

He wished he never had to see the rotten place again.

Chapter 3

The Mystery Bean

In the morning Mum gave Tom a look when he put two spoons of sugar on his Frosties. "Those flakes have sugar on already, Tom," she said. She hadn't heated up any baked beans to go with his bacon and eggs, so he had to heat them up himself.

"I'll go on a diet next week, Mum," explained Tom. "When I'm back at school. I need my food right now."

Mum gave a sigh. Molly just laughed.

Dad wasn't in the kitchen. He was talking on his Experiment House security phone, and walking up and down the garden.

He came in just as Tom had finished eating.

"What's happened?" said Tom. "I saw lights and cars up at Experiment House last night. Should I stay at home?"

"Just a mix-up," said Dad. "You can carry on with your work experience. But you stay in the filing room, OK?"

"What if I need to go to the toilet?"

"There are toilets by the canteen. Don't leave that corridor."

Tom wondered if he'd have to wear the baby-suit again.

He did have to wear the horrible Clean-Suit. And Tom was too scared of Mrs Stevens to beg her to let him keep his own clothes on.

There was a lot more filing in the basket on the desk.

Tom didn't want to do *anything*, except maybe die – in a way that didn't hurt.

Experiment House had been silent on his first day. Today he could hear phones ringing, bleepers bleeping, worried voices, footsteps hurrying up and down the corridors. But he didn't even care. No one came near Tom's room. He stared at the blank white walls, and the boring cabinets and desk, and thought about Alison. He was so lonely. He knew that food would comfort him, but all he had was his lunch. After that, he'd have nothing left. His dad had told him not to leave his corridor today. No canteen then …

Then he saw the chocolate bean. It was lying on the floor under a radiator. Just a piece of chocolate, without a wrapper. Not many people would have seen it, but Tom had

sharp eyes. At first he pretended that he
hadn't seen it. Then he got down on the floor
to have a closer look. The filing room was
very clean – there was no dust under the
radiator. The bean was about as big as Tom's
thumb. It was creamy brown and slightly
lumpy, as if there were chopped nuts or bits
of toffee in the chocolate.

Poor old bean, thought Tom. *No one will
enjoy you now.*

Tom knew it wasn't good to eat something
that had been on the floor. But he couldn't
help it. The bean seemed to call to him. His
hand stretched out and picked it up. The
bean looked very, very delicious ... Tom took
it back to the table. Someone knocked on the
door, and then came in. It was Mrs Stevens,
with a tray. Tom shoved the bean into his
lunch-box.

"Here's a cup of tea for you," said Mrs
Stevens and smiled. "I thought I'd make sure

you were all right. The whole place is in a panic. You won't see your dad this morning! He's with Dr Wilson right now."

"What's going on?" asked Tom but he didn't much care.

"Ooh, I couldn't tell you," said Mrs Stevens. "Would you like a biscuit?"

"No, thank you," said Tom.

Mrs Stevens grinned. "On a diet, dear? That's a good idea."

"I'm *not* on a diet," said Tom. "I'm just not hungry."

He felt as if everyone in the world was laughing at him.

"Don't go into the corridors," she said, as she left. "Stay in here."

I don't want to go anywhere, thought Tom. *I hate Experiment House.*

The tea had no sugar in it. He thought of the chocolate bean, and felt it calling to him. But he would be strong, he wouldn't eat something that had been on the floor.

I'll throw it away at lunchtime, he told himself. *When I open my lunch-box. I'm not as greedy as that.*

Chapter 4

The Lunch That Vanished

Tom drank his tea. He drank the bottle of juice that was meant to go with his lunch. He went to the toilet. But he couldn't stop thinking about that delicious bean. At 10.30 he opened his lunch-box, and got a terrible shock.

It was empty.

There was nothing left in it except the chocolate bean.

Tom was puzzled. He knew his lunch had been in there. He had watched his mum put the sandwiches in his box. And an apple, and a piece of flapjack. *Maybe I dozed off*, he thought. *Did I eat my lunch in my sleep?*

But then why would he feel so *hungry*!

The chocolate bean looked at Tom. It had no eyes, but it was looking at him.

There's something weird going on, thought Tom. He shut the box and went to look out of the door. He could see two people in white coats at the front desk. They were talking to the security guards and they weren't looking Tom's way. He crept out, in his awful baby-suit. He had a 50p that he'd put in the pocket of the baby-suit when he got changed. He'd be able to buy a chocolate bar. He went to the vending machine outside the canteen, bought a bar, and hurried back to the filing room.

The chocolate bar made his mouth water. He wanted it but he had to give it up. He took off the wrapper, put the bar in his lunch-box with the bean, and shut the box. He waited for half an hour, then he opened the box. The time had gone by fast. Tom was so keen to see if his weird idea was true, he forgot about being hungry.

The chocolate bar had gone. The bean sat there, all alone.

Tom looked at the bean. The bean looked at Tom.

It hadn't changed. It wasn't bigger, it wasn't lumpier.

But Tom had *proved* that his weird idea was right.

All my lunch is inside that bean, thought Tom.

And he was starving.

Eat me!

Tom couldn't hear the words, but *he knew* what the bean wanted.

His hand reached out. The bean felt warm and silky.

It smelled like the best sort of rich, creamy chocolate.

Tom put it in his mouth.

Nothing happened.

****

After a few minutes, Tom thought, *That's funny. I don't feel hungry any more.* Then he started on the huge stack of filing. The work went quickly. It was even fun, once he got down to it. He found out that if he opened all the drawers in the steel cabinets, he could toss the papers into them from across the room. At first not many papers went into the right folders, but he got better at the game. It was fun, and interesting.

It was odd, but he didn't feel lonely any more.

Half-way through the afternoon there was another knock on the door. It was his dad, with Dr Wilson himself.

"Hello, Tom," said the boss of Experiment House. "How are you getting on?"

"Great!" said Tom. He should have felt embarrassed, because he was dressed in the horrible Clean-Suit and he'd been throwing the papers around. But he didn't. "My score is going up and up."

He told Dr Wilson how he'd made the filing into a game.

Dad looked worried, but Dr Wilson laughed.

"You're a bright boy," he said. "You're the kind of young man I like! I wish I could give you a better look at our work here, but I'm sorry to say I've got some bad news –"

Dr Wilson told Tom that he couldn't finish his work experience. Something had come up.

"Only people who work for the government can be here now," he said.

"I'm sorry, Tom," said Tom's dad. "It just didn't work out. You'd better go and get changed, and then I'll take you home."

****

For the next few days the family almost never saw Tom's dad. He had to work extra hours, and he had to drive Dr Wilson to important meetings, which meant he was away overnight. Other odd things happened. Police vans were parked on street corners, helicopters rattled in the sky. People spotted soldiers in army trucks in the countryside around Experiment House. The TV news said they were carrying out a 'routine exercise', and that no one need worry, but Tom's dad looked worried all the time.

Tom and Molly were afraid their dad might be in trouble.

One night at dinner Molly asked him what was going on. "Dad," she said, "has there been a break-in at Experiment House? Are you going to lose your job?"

"No," he said. "It's nothing like that. Everything's fine, it's just the scientists in a flap about nothing."

Tom was glad his dad wasn't in trouble. Ever since he'd eaten the bean, Tom himself had been feeling great.

His life had changed. He didn't care who laughed at him, he wasn't lonely any more. It was as if he had a new friend, someone who liked food as much as Tom did. And the friend had never tasted any of Tom's favourite things before. Tom had been saving money for Alison's birthday present. Now he spent it on treats. Pork pie with french mustard, lamb and chicken kebabs, chunky chips with mayo ... One day he ate a whole tub of cherry and cheesecake ice-cream, on the way home from school.

But he felt full of energy, not full of food, and when he stepped on the scales his weight hadn't gone up. It had gone down. Quite a bit.

He wasn't afraid, but it was *weird*.

Chapter 5
The Night Shift

Two weeks went by. The extra police and the soldiers left. There were no more reports on the news. Everything went back to normal – except for Tom. Then Dad came home grumbling. He had to go on night shift. Tom's dad didn't often do nights because he was the head of security. But a lot of the guards were taking time off, because of all the extra hours they'd worked when the big panic was on. Tom had an idea. He could tell his dad was in a good mood, even if he was grumbling. If Tom could go to Experiment

House at night, he could have a look around. He wanted to find out something about his bean.

"Dad, is there any chance that I could do a night shift with you? I really need to finish my work experience this month. It's important, it goes on my records."

"They don't want you back there," said Molly. "They threw you out, fatso."

"No one threw me out!" protested Tom.

"It would be good for him, Dan," said Mum. "He didn't make any fuss when he had to stop his work experience, but it was a shame."

Dad thought about it. "I'll ask Dr Wilson," he said. "It should be OK. There's nothing going on in the labs right now, and Dr Wilson thought you were great, Tom."

"Dad," said Molly, "what *happened*?" She was always the nosey one of the family.

"Why were all the soldiers around? Can you tell us *anything*?"

Mum frowned. "Molly! You know he can't talk about work."

Dad laughed. "I can't tell you anything, because I don't *know* anything. I think it was all a false alarm. All right, Tom," Dad went on, "I'll see about that night shift. I'll try to make it Friday, so you can sleep in on Saturday morning."

"*Yes!*" cried Tom. "Excellent!" And he made a face at Molly.

"He's been very good at keeping to his diet, too," said Mum.

"No, he hasn't!" cried Molly. "He's been eating like a pig, same as always."

"I have not!"

"You *have*! You even eat too much when it's *broccoli* –"

"I don't eat like a pig, I eat like someone who likes his food," said Tom. "I *like* broccoli because it tastes good. Hot with melted butter, or cold with mayo, and it's nice fried in olive oil, with a fried egg –"

Molly stuck her fingers in her ears. "You're disgusting. Shut up! Shut up!"

"Shush, both of you," said Mum. "You're giving me a headache."

****

Dr Wilson said it would be OK for Tom to go on the night shift with his dad. Dad warned Tom that it would be boring. But it turned out to be fun. Tom didn't have to stay in the filing room. Before Dad went off to the security control room, he took Tom to the supply room. The first uniform they tried fitted him. "There you go," Dad said. "You're not as fat as all that. Shirley Stevens was messing around when she made you wear that Clean-Suit."

Then he left Tom with the friendly guards on the front desk.

They showed Tom how to use the CCTV. He wasn't allowed to go on patrol, but he talked to the patrolmen on the radio-phone. One of the guards, a big woman called Lauren, was very funny, like a stand-up comedian. She fooled about and kept everyone laughing.

At midnight Tom had to take a two-hour break and get some sleep.

"It's against the rules for a kid like you to work all night," said Lauren.

Everyone laughed, because Tom hadn't been *working*. He'd been playing mini-basketball with paper balls and a pot noodle container that was stuck up on top of a door frame, and flicking elastic bands down the empty corridors, like everyone else.

"When the cat's away, the mice will play," said another guard, called Ravi.

Tom wondered who "the cat" was. Did they mean Dr Wilson was away? But he didn't ask. You can't ask too many questions in a Top Secret place.

The rest room was on the same corridor as the supply room, and the room where Tom had done his filing. There were camp beds with blankets, and a fridge, a microwave and a sink. Ravi took Tom along there. Tom switched off the light and lay down. The floodlights from outside shone into the room. Tom didn't feel tired. He was wide awake, and this was his chance. As soon as he was sure Ravi had gone, he got up and put his uniform jacket back on.

He picked up his torch and shone it as he looked at himself in the rest room mirror. In the shadowy mirror he looked like a real security guard, just the way he'd dreamed of looking. He knew he had lost a lot of weight.

And he certainly *hadn't* been on a diet.

It was a mystery.

"I've been worrying a lot," he said, aloud. "That's what it is."

It wasn't true. He hadn't been worrying at all.

Chapter 6

Lindy

Tom made up his mind to go upstairs to the labs. He knew there were some stairs around the corner by the canteen, so he wouldn't have to pass the front desk. He also knew where the security cameras were. If he kept out of sight, he wouldn't show up on the CCTV screens. He should be able to get past the scan at the doors to the back stairs, because his ID was recorded in the system.

He didn't know exactly *what* he was looking for. All he knew was that he had found the bean in this building. He shone his torch under the radiators as he went along, just in case there was another one …

He stopped at the doors to the stairs. What if the alarms went off when he walked through the scan? *Maybe this is stupid*, thought Tom. Then something made him look out of the window, and a thrill of excitement shot through him. He could see a dark figure climbing up the wall of Experiment House.

That's impossible! thought Tom. How could anyone have got over the huge fence, past the guard patrol and the dogs, through all the infra-red beams? Alarms should have been ringing everywhere. But there wasn't a sound.

Tom had to stop the intruder. The windows were locked, but he'd seen a set of keys to the ground floor windows in the guards' rest room. He raced back there, grabbed the keys, opened the window and dived out into the night. He picked himself up, and ran around the corner of the building. The intruder was still climbing.

"Hey!" he shouted. The figure dropped to the ground and ran for it.

Tom knew he shouldn't handle this on his own. But it was too late. If Tom went for help now, the intruder would get away. The dark figure might have a weapon, but Tom would have to take the risk ... All this went through his mind in less than a moment, as he sprinted across the lawns. He flung himself at the person. He'd never liked rugby, but he tried to make it like a flying tackle, and it worked! Tom was amazed. He was bigger and heavier than the intruder. He had soon pinned his enemy to the ground, but the intruder kept up the struggle and kicked him in the back.

"Just knock that off!" gasped Tom. "Or I'll call the dogs!"

He made the intruder stand up and didn't let go as he pulled off the black hood. It was a girl – the same age as him!

"Who are you?" he shouted. "What are you doing, breaking in here?"

"I won't tell you! I don't care what you do. You're one of them. *Torturer*!"

"What do you mean? I'm hardly even hurting you."

"That's what they do here," she snarled. "They're torturers for the government. And you're one of them. You work for the evil Dr Wilson."

"Shut up," snapped Tom. "My dad works here. He wouldn't torture anyone."

"Yes, he would. Go on, then, you brute. Take me to your officer."

Tom wasn't sure. He'd captured an intruder, just the way he'd dreamed. But she was only a girl. If he handed her over to the guards, they'd call the police. What if she was sent to prison, and it was Tom's fault? He didn't like that idea. And he wanted to know why she had called his dad a torturer.

"Come with me," he said, in a deep, gruff voice, and kept a tight hold of her arm. "I want to ask you some questions. But I warn you – if you yell, or if you try to escape, I'll set the dogs on you right away."

Tom marched the girl back to the open window of the rest room, and told her to climb inside. She looked at him.

"What – !" she said.

"Just do as I say," growled Tom.

He held her arm again, locked the window and, this time, he closed the blinds.

Then he switched the light on.

She stared at him. "You're not a guard! You're just a kid!"

"My name's Tom," said Tom, in his normal voice. "But never mind who I am. You're in big trouble. Tell me who you are and what you're doing here."

The girl was wearing black jeans and a black jacket. Her red curly hair sprang out around her head. She had freckles on her nose. She didn't look very dangerous.

"My name's Lindy. I'm an Alien Rights Activist."

Tom didn't understand. "What are you talking about?" he said.

"You don't know what goes on in the labs at all, do you?" said Lindy. "Well, I'll tell you. About a year ago, the government captured an alien, from another planet. They stole its spaceship, and they're keeping it here as a prisoner. They're torturing an innocent

51

Extra-Terrestrial, who came to our world in peace. *Right here in Experiment House –"*

"You're kidding," said Tom. "Or else you're nuts. You've been watching too much TV. My dad is chief of security here. He's never said anything about aliens!"

"Don't be stupid. Of course he hasn't told you. It's Top Secret."

"I don't believe you. Experiment House is just some kind of boring, harmless government science place."

"That's what they want you to think. Do you think they'd have a big notice on the gates, saying ALIENS TORTURED HERE?"

"I'm going to take you to my dad. I gave you a chance to explain –"

Lindy looked scared. "I can prove it!" she burst out. She pulled a shiny plastic card from her jeans pocket. "I'll show you. This keycard will get us into the labs."

"Where did you get that!" cried Tom.

"We have contacts," said Lindy. "Do you dare to come with me?"

So Tom went with her. She had called his dad a torturer: Tom had to know the truth. He could turn her in later ...

Lindy knew how to avoid the security cameras, and she wasn't afraid of the scan at the doors to the back stairs. She walked right up the stairs. No alarms went off. Tom began to feel worried. This girl wasn't a harmless nutter. She could fool the security system. She really was some kind of terrorist.

It felt weird upstairs at Experiment House. Tom hadn't been up there before, but he knew the lab work never closed down. Even at night, machines should be humming, and lights should be glowing. Instead everything felt empty and shut down, as if the scientists had left forever. It was easy opening the top-security locks with Lindy's keycard. But when the two of them went into the labs, there was nothing but computer monitors and towers and they were all switched off, all dark and dead.

"What's going on?" muttered Lindy. "It's not meant to be like this."

"Told you so," said Tom. "It's just harmless government science. Everyone's gone home for the weekend." But he knew that wasn't right. The hair on the back of his neck began to prickle. He felt very spooked, but he didn't really know why.

Every time they went into a lab, they made sure the blinds were closed, and then Tom shone his big torch around. At last they came to a room that looked more like a science lab at school. There were test tubes and electrical things lined up on the counters.

There was a glass case standing on a table, with something glittery inside it.

Lindy gasped. "There it is!" she hissed.

Tom had kept one of her arms twisted up behind her back, so she couldn't get away. He didn't let go. Lindy stepped across the room towards the glass case and she pulled Tom with her.

They looked into the case.

There was a space capsule inside, almost like the NASA one Tom had once seen in the Science Museum in London, on a school trip. It was round and silver, with coils, spikes and saucers like satellite dishes all over the outside. It had been cut in half, so Lindy and Tom could see into it. Inside there was a control panel, and a sort of couch with safety bars, to keep the pilot strapped in.

It looked like the real thing. Except that it was no bigger than a grapefruit.

"So what happened?" said Tom. "Did the scientists *shrink* it?" He was being sarcastic.

"No," said Lindy, in a serious voice. "That's the size the alien ship was when it landed. Aliens don't have to be huge monsters."

"Don't be stupid. It's a toy!" said Tom.

"Oh, yeah?" said Lindy. "So why is it here? In this Top Secret lab?" She looked around her, as best she could with her arm twisted behind her back. "But I don't like this. Why is everything closed down? Tom, listen to me, this is very weird. We know that Dr Wilson is in London, talking to the Prime Minister –"

Tom was shocked. "The Prime Minister! You're *kidding*!"

"Yes. We didn't know why. I just thought it was a good chance to break in. Now I'm scared. Tom, I think they must have killed the alien!"

Tom kept a tight hold on Lindy's wrist, but he was staring at the tiny spaceship.

He thought about the police, the army trucks and the helicopters. All those people must have been looking for something. Something that had escaped?

He remembered the night he'd looked out and seen the searchlights from his bedroom window.

He remembered what had happened to him the next day ...

Lindy didn't notice that Tom had gone very quiet.

"You realise what this means?" she said. "We'll be invaded! The first alien came in peace, now there'll be war. They may be tiny, but they could have super-weapons. They could be on their way already and they'll want revenge ..."

Tom looked at the little couch with the safety bars. The dent in the cushion was a shape he knew. It was almost like a bean. He felt sick.

"I don't think the alien's dead, Lindy. Er, I think it escaped."

She twisted around. "So you *do* know something!" she cried. "Tom, we could all be in terrible danger! You have to tell me what you know!"

Chapter 7
The Writing On The Wall

Tom had begun to feel very, very weird. It was as if there were words that he had to say, but he had forgotten how to talk. His mouth began to move on its own, and groaning, choking noises came up from his throat –

"Tom! What's wrong?" asked Lindy. "Stop that! Say something!"

Tom couldn't answer. The groaning noises stopped. Now it was as if something had taken over his arms and legs. He *had to* leave the lab. Lindy tried to stop him. She tried to tell him they must lock the doors again, or the security system would know there'd been intruders. But Tom *had to* rush back to the ground floor. He needed to head for the front desk, to get help. But he couldn't. He *had to* take Lindy to the little room where he had done the filing.

The thing inside him made him shut the door and turn the light on.

Lindy rubbed her arms. "What are we doing in here?"

Tom didn't know. He couldn't say. He just *had to* shove the filing cabinets out of the way. A wastepaper bin went flying and scattered scrap paper everywhere. Then he grabbed two chairs, and shoved Lindy down on one of them. The power inside flung Tom into the chair next to her. He felt that his arms and legs were his own again but he didn't dare move.

Lindy and Tom were staring at a blank white wall.

"What's going on?" whispered Lindy.

Tom moaned in fear. "Sssh! I have to look at the wall!"

The white wall was like a movie screen without a picture.

Tom stared until his head began to spin.

And slowly, the letters started to appear.

Something, some power from inside Tom, was writing on the wall.

Please

"Wow!" whispered Lindy. "Are you *doing* that, Tom?"

"Watch the wall," croaked Tom.

Please, Please, *Please* don't throw me out ...

I thought we were friends

I won't do you any harm –

"Wow!" Lindy was stunned. "Is that *the alien*? Is the alien in contact with your mind? Is it speaking through you? Incredible! You're so lucky!"

Tom shook his head, and stared at the wall. He had to keep looking at the wall. He knew he mustn't move.

Lindy clutched her head, as if she was trying to help her brain to take this in.

"Fantastic! I have to ask it things. This is fantastic." She sat up straight, and took a deep breath. "Who are you? Can you tell me who you are?" she began.

I'm not dead! said the writing on the wall. **You call me the alien, but that's not my name. I'm "zy%"*88cx!>"**.

"Where are you now? I'm here to rescue you!" Lindy asked next.

No, thanks. I'm very happy where I am.

"But you could be in danger. You have to tell me where you are!"

All right ... If you must know, I'm inside Tom.

The writing on the wall vanished. Lindy looked at Tom. Her eyes were big as saucers. Her mouth had dropped open in horror and amazement.

"It's true. I ate the alien," said Tom.

Now he knew what had happened. He had guessed the truth when he saw the couch in the tiny spaceship. It had been just big enough for an alien creature that looked like a chocolate bean ...

The alien had escaped from the lab, but it hadn't been able to get out of Experiment House. It had hidden under the radiator in this filing room.

And Tom had found it.

Now he understood that feeling he'd had when he'd eaten the bean, the feeling that he was not alone –

"I thought it was a chocolate! I didn't know it was an alien!" Lindy was looking more and more shocked. "I only swallowed it," Tom told her. "I didn't *chew* –!"

They heard footsteps in the corridor outside. Lindy dived behind the filing cabinets. The door opened and there was Tom's dad.

"Tom?" he said. "What are you doing in here?"

"Chocolate –" said Tom. It was the first thing that came into his head.

Dad stared at the waste bin on the floor and the paper all over the room. He looked at the two chairs in the middle of the room and the filing cabinets pushed to one side.

"I, er, I remembered I'd left a chocolate bar in here," babbled Tom. "When I was doing the filing. I was looking for it –"

"Trust you," Tom's dad said with a sigh. "Well, come on. Leave this, I'll lock up and the cleaners will see to it in the morning."

"I can't!" Tom was horrified. *What would happen to Lindy?* "You go ahead, Dad. I won't be long. I've just got to, er, find my chocolate!"

Dad shook his head. "I just told you, Tom, you have to come with me. If you're so desperate, I'll get you another bar from the vending machine."

There was nothing Tom could do.

Chapter 8
The Activists

The next evening, Tom was in his room. Nothing more had happened. The creature inside him hadn't been writing on any walls, and it hadn't taken over his body again. He felt as if it was hiding in a corner inside him, trembling with fear. But Tom was very scared himself. It was difficult to be sure if the alien was feeling so scared or just him.

He'd tried to tell himself this was all a bad dream, but he knew it wasn't.

He'd bought a pack of biscuits, a six-pack of fruit yoghurt, a bag of mixed chocolate bars, some bananas and some apples. He'd smuggled it all up here in his school bag. He sat on his bed, eating and eating. Tom didn't taste any of it. But he felt a bit less scared when all the biscuits, two yoghurts, three bananas and three apples were inside him.

He couldn't bear to eat the chocolate.

He'd have to get more supplies. He didn't dare stop eating – he'd have to keep eating forever.

It was like a terrible punishment for loving food too much.

Something rapped on his window. Tom went and peered out. He saw a slim figure in the garden, hiding in the shadows by the wheely bin. He knew who it must be. Lindy must have escaped. He would have to let her in, before anyone spotted her. Why couldn't she just knock on the door? He went down to the back door and let her into the kitchen.

"How did you get away?" he asked.

"I'm highly trained," said Lindy. "Tom, I have to talk to you."

Then Tom's mum came into the kitchen.

"Oh, hello," she said, with a big smile. "Who's this, Tom?"

"Just a friend," muttered Tom.

"That's *nice*," said Mum. "What lovely red hair. What's your name, dear?"

"I'm Lindy," she said.

"What a pretty name! I bet you two would like a snack. Cheese on toast –?"

Tom loved cheese on toast. Cheddar cheese, with a blob of pickle on top. He would have been embarrassed if Lindy had been a girl he liked. Mum made it sound as if all

Tom thought about was food. But he didn't care now.

He shook his head, and shuddered.

"No, thanks. Let's go up to my room, Lindy."

As they went into his room, Tom saw himself in the mirror on his wardrobe door. His hair was sticking up on end, his eyes were wild. His cheeks, which had been so plump and pink two weeks ago, were pale and hollow. He looked like someone on the run from the police.

Lindy stared at what was left of Tom's feast.

"*You've* been having a party," she said.

"It isn't funny," wailed Tom. "The alien has been eating my food, from inside me. I've lost a lot of weight already. I'm afraid if I stop eating, it will start to eat *me*."

Lindy looked him over. "How much weight have you lost? You don't look thin."

"Two weeks ago I was *fat*," said Tom, grimly. "My parents think I've been on a diet, but *I haven't*. What's happening *isn't natural*."

"Oh." Tom could see Lindy didn't believe him. "Well, anyway," she said, "you have to come and meet my group. I've told them what happened at Experiment House. That writing on the wall was so weird. We have to find out if the alien is really inside you."

"What will you do then?" asked Tom, bitterly. "Cut me open and rescue it?"

Lindy's face went white, so her freckles stood out like dark stars. "I don't know, Tom. Maybe ... maybe something like that. It might be the only way to save your life."

The alien doesn't want to be rescued, thought Tom. He thought of the bean digging deeper into his insides, and the Activists going after it with sharp knives –

He had that weird feeling again, but much worse.

The bean was trying to take him over again. It didn't want him to go with Lindy.

He fought the feeling down. "OK," he gasped at last. "Take me to the Alien Rights Activists. Quickly, because I'm losing control."

"We're just going to my house," Lindy shouted into the kitchen as they ran out.

There was a car waiting round the corner, a big dark car, parked without lights. Lindy and Tom got into the back. Tom could only see the outlines of the people in front. He watched the lights of his home town passing by, and tried to stop his hands from pulling at the door handle. What would it feel like to be eaten from the inside? Would the alien eat his bones? Would there be nothing left at the end but a bag of dry skin, like an empty crisp packet?

Lindy didn't say a word, and nor did the people in the front of the car. A kind of sobbing tried to get out of Tom's throat, but he swallowed it.

He was so scared. But the most horrible thing was that he felt as if his friend the bean was begging him not to betray it –

He didn't know where they were going until he saw the big, bright signs of a hospital. The car drove through the gates, and through a maze of car parks to a block on its own. Everything outside was dark and still.

"We get out here," said Lindy, in a nervous voice.

A man and a woman got out of the front of the car. They looked at Tom and smiled, but he could see they weren't sure about what he'd told Lindy. The bean tried to make Tom run away. But Lindy took his hand. It was good to feel her grip. The man and woman took them down a corridor. Tom saw a sign on the wall saying MRI Scanning Department, with a pointing arrow. He wondered what MRI meant.

The bean had gone quiet. It had given up fighting.

Tom had thought Lindy's 'group' would look like nutters. He was shocked when he saw six very serious, important-looking grown-up men and women. One of the women was wearing a doctor's white coat. Everyone sat down. The room they were in smelled of hospitals. *This is where they cut me open*, thought Tom, and cold sweat ran down his back.

One of the men had wild, curly red hair that was going grey. He had freckles, too. He looked like a little boy, but old and wise at the same time. "Tom," he said, "I'm Greg Taylor, I'm Lindy's father. And you're Tom Brooks. Your dad is Dan Brooks, head of security at Experiment House?"

Tom nodded.

"Lindy has told us your story. We didn't know she was going to break into Experiment House, by the way. I don't want you to think I'd have let my daughter do that –"

"Someone had to do it," muttered Lindy.

"I'm Dr Margaret Lee," said the woman in the white coat. "I work at the hospital. This is my department. That's why we can use this room. Tom, we want to take a scan of your body. It won't hurt, and it won't do you any harm –"

Tom suddenly felt even more scared. "You ... you mean *you believe me*?"

"I'm one of the people who studied the alien visitor," said Lindy's father. "I was one of the leaders of the science team. Dr Wilson was the other. About six months ago we fell out and I left Experiment House. I know something about what kind of creature this alien is." He looked very serious. "In answer to your question, yes, Tom. I think it could have been trying to look like food."

"My dad thinks the alien works like a plant," said Lindy. "Like plants on earth that grow bright, sweet fruit, so animals will eat the fruit and spread their seeds."

"The alien's not a plant," said Tom. "It's a person."

The Alien Rights Activists looked at each other.

"Tom," said Lindy's dad, "is the alien listening to us now?"

"Yes," said Tom.

"Will it hurt you if we take a scan to see if it's really in your stomach?"

Tom felt the bean take over. It made him move his head from side to side, slowly.

No.

"I think we should go ahead," said Dr Lee. "Tom, if it wants us to stop, just squeeze this button at any time."

Tom had to take everything metal out of his pockets, and take his belt off because of the buckle. He'd lost so much weight that his trousers almost fell down when he took his belt off. He lay on the bed of the scanning machine and held tight onto his alarm button. There was a soft buzzing sound. The bed moved into the scanner, and Tom was swallowed up by a grey tunnel. He heard Lindy saying, "I can't look!"

He heard Dr Lee shout, "My God! *There it is*!"

He couldn't feel a thing, but the Activists must be looking at his insides.

"It's in his stomach!" said Lindy's dad's voice. "And it's alive."

The bed slid out of the scanner. Tom gave a moan. He sat up, and pointed wildly at the wall of the exam room. He couldn't speak.

"This is what happened before!" cried Lindy. "The alien writes messages on the wall!"

The Activists did what the bean wanted them to do. They moved a cabinet so that there was a space on the wall, and the alien wrote its message.

Please don't cut Tom open!

Tom is my friend.

I only eat food he doesn't need.

I'm sens-dimensing it home to my planet. We need more food.

I can only do this from inside Tom.

Please! All we want is a little of your tasty food.

The alien was getting better at writing on walls. It wrote very quickly, and the words didn't fade.

"The words will stay as long as I look at the wall," said Tom.

"This is *serious*," said Lindy's dad at last. "Time for a change of plan."

"I thought you liked aliens," Tom said, and he looked at Lindy's dad. The lines of writing vanished at once. "I thought you wanted to protect it."

The Alien Rights Activists said nothing, but their faces were grave. Tom knew what they were thinking. Anything they said to Tom, the bean could hear.

He felt very, very scared.

Chapter 9
Interview With An Alien

Lindy's dad rang Tom's parents, and asked if Tom could stay at Lindy's overnight. Mum insisted on talking to Tom, but she wasn't worried. She just wanted to tell Tom to be nice, so Lindy's parents wouldn't be sorry they invited him.

"Tom," she said. "I don't want to embarrass you, but ... don't overeat!"

If only you knew, thought Tom.

Lindy's mum was an Activist too. She acted so sorry for Tom that he felt even more scared. Maybe she knew things the others hadn't told him. She gave him a big supply of tempting food to take to bed with him, in case the alien got hungry.

Tom couldn't eat. He felt as if the bean couldn't eat either. He lay awake in the Taylors' spare room. Why hadn't the government told anyone about the alien? *It's wrong to lie to us*, he thought. *This is our world, we should all decide what to do about an alien visitor.* He tried to send the bean a message of friendship, so it wouldn't attack him.

They won't hurt you, he thought. *They wouldn't dare!*

He didn't know if the bean understood. It felt very small and frightened. He thought of the spaceship that had been cut in half, and that made him feel sorry for the invader inside him. Poor bean. What if it really didn't mean any harm?

****

Lindy's dad must have called Dr Wilson. The next day Lindy's dad, Tom, Lindy and Dr Lee all went to Experiment House. Tom was very glad Lindy was allowed to come along. Dr Wilson met them at the front desk.

Tom's dad was there too, in his smart uniform.

"What's going on, Tom?" said his dad.

"I'm not sure," said Tom.

"We need to talk to you, Mr Brooks," said Lindy's dad.

The adults walked away and put their heads together. Tom and Lindy stayed by the desk. In a few minutes the three scientists and Tom's dad came back. Dad was looking horrified. But he wasn't looking *surprised*.

"You knew about the alien, didn't you," said Tom.

"It was Top Secret, son. I never dreamed you'd get mixed up in it like this! My God! It's all my fault! I wish I'd never let you come here –"

"It's OK, dad," said Tom. "Keep calm. I'll be fine."

"All right," said Dad. "The experts here say you'll be OK. They seem to know how, er, how our alien friend works. I love you, Tom."

Tom nodded. He was too choked to say anything.

Lindy got hold of Tom's hand, and glared at the grown-ups.

"I'm staying with him."

Tom saw that Lindy knew something he didn't. Something had been decided. No one had told him, because anything they told Tom, the bean would hear.

Lindy and Tom waited in Dr Wilson's office. "Are you scared?" asked Lindy.

"Not really," said Tom. "Not any more."

He was beyond being scared. Everything was like a dream.

Dr Wilson, Professor Taylor and Dr Lee had gone to the labs. They came back with three lab workers. Two of them had brought a big smart board. Another woman was pushing a metal trolley with a cover.

Tom wondered what was under there.

"Tom," said Dr Wilson. "Is your alien partner ready to talk to us?"

Tom didn't have to answer. The alien made him nod his head.

Everyone sat down and looked at the smart board. It was like a private movie show.

This time they all knew what to expect.

All right, I'll talk, said the writing on the wall. **Please don't hurt me**.

"We mean you no harm," said Dr Wilson. "We've been trying to talk to you for months. We didn't know you had to be inside someone. Why did you come to Earth?"

We have not enough food. You have spare food. I can send food back to my world from inside Tom, by sens-dimensing it.

"Could you explain exactly what you mean by that?" Dr Wilson asked.

There was a long wait.

I can't tell you. I can only explain things that Tom understands.

"I see," said Dr Wilson. Tom knew the scientists were looking at each other, passing silent messages. But he had to keep looking at the wall or the writing would vanish.

"You say you won't hurt Tom, and you only take the food he doesn't need. You've made him lose weight. What if you were inside someone thin, who didn't have any food stored as fat. What would happen then?"

I like the things Tom eats, wrote the bean. **But I can make food from anything on your planet. Or I can eat things you throw away. I would make my thin friend healthy and strong by changing your "rubbish" into food for him. Or her.**

"Amazing," murmured Professor Taylor.

"Just think," whispered Dr Lee. "The answer to world hunger!"

Dr Wilson asked another question.

"What if we were to accept your mission. What would happen then?"

More of us would come, and be stomach guests. We would come and live inside your people.

"How many more aliens would come?"

We're not aliens. We may look different, but we're people just like you. I don't know how many of us would come. Living inside a big creature's stomach, on another planet, is not everyone's idea of fun. We ask for volunteers.

"Could you guess how many?"

There was another long wait.

Maybe a few million?

"I see," said Dr Wilson. "And these stomach guests would do no harm?"

I would never, never, never hurt my friend. That would be worse than murder. We love our food.

The scientists were silent for what seemed like a long time. Tom wished he knew what they were thinking. Were they going to allow the aliens to come to earth?

Dr Wilson said, "Have you told your people where you are?"

I haven't told them how to get here yet. It didn't seem safe when you were keeping me prisoner. But I can do it. It's easy.

Then Dr Lee said, "We want to do something more now. We want to give Tom a drug, so you can use his mind freely, and explain things he couldn't understand. Will you agree to that, alien friend –?"

My name's "zy%"*88cx!>". But you can call me Zock. All right, I agree. But don't hurt Tom!

"Thank you, Zock," said Professor Taylor. "I promise we won't hurt Tom."

Tom had to lie on a couch and roll up his sleeve. Dr Lee rubbed his arm with something cold, and then came the little prick of the injection. Almost at once he started feeling woozy. But he knew the bean felt woozy too. The *bean* was falling asleep. It wouldn't be able to talk to them! He wanted to tell the scientists, but everything felt far away. Dr Lee bent over him, and passed a thing like a silver saucer over his chest. He heard her say, "OK, it's under. Our friend is in deep sleep."

"Let's get on with this," said Dr Wilson's voice.

The metal trolley was near the couch. The cover was gone. Tom saw something like a slim metal snake. At one end of the snake there was a TV monitor. At the other end, there was a red camera eye, and shiny grabbing jaws.

Tom felt fuzzy. He was almost asleep. Lindy was holding his hand. Dr Lee's voice asked him to open his mouth. They wanted Tom to swallow the metal snake. He didn't care. He opened his mouth and the snake went in. Its jaws were folded up like the petals of a flower. The metal snake slid down his throat.

Dr Lee worked the controls on the monitor, and watched what the camera eye could see. She talked softly to the other scientists. Her voice was a soothing buzz. The bean didn't know what was happening, it couldn't hide, it was asleep. Tom thought the snake was like one of those machines you get in a fairground. You put in your money and you have to guide some claws to pick up a toy. You try to make the claws pick up the toy you want to have ...

Chapter 10
The Alien Defeated

Tom came round slowly, and opened his eyes. His throat hurt. The metal trolley with the horrible metal snake had gone. Lindy was still holding his hand. Dr Wilson was there too. Lindy had a big smile and Dr Wilson looked much happier.

"Are you all right, Tom?"

"I think so," croaked Tom. "What happened? What did you do?"

"Drink this," said Dr Wilson. "It'll make your throat feel better."

Tom sat up and drank something sweet and smooth. He lay back and stared at the ceiling. His head was still woozy, but he knew that the bean was gone.

"You took it out, didn't you?" Tom asked.

"Yes, we did, Tom."

"I thought you were going to talk to Zock without me –"

"I'm afraid that was a trick," Dr Wilson said.

Dr Lee and Professor Taylor came back into the room.

Professor Taylor said, "Tom, remember I told you how I worked at Experiment House before? We were very frustrated, because we couldn't talk to the alien. We didn't know if it was a person, an animal, or some kind of machine. Dr Wilson wanted to start internal experiments. That means he wanted to cut the alien open. I knew that was wrong, and I was sure it was dangerous –"

"Zock's people would have come to get revenge," said Lindy.

"Maybe they would," agreed Lindy's dad. "So I became the leader of the Alien Rights Activists. But now we know the truth. The aliens think of humans as *food*. That's what 'Zock' said: '*We love our food.*' These aliens are very dangerous."

"What about Zock? Where is he? What will you do to him?"

"We won't harm it," said Dr Wilson. "We'll continue our investigation. But we think you should see these photos, Tom. This is what your 'chocolate bean' looked like, before it escaped and went to look for someone's stomach to live in."

Tom looked at the black and white photos. The alien was a coiled-up, whiteish worm, with a hooked mouth and little caterpillar legs. It looked nasty.

The adults left Tom alone with Lindy.

Tom sat up, and put his head in his hands. "I feel as if I betrayed my friend," he said. "Zock really didn't do me any harm."

"I know what you mean," said Lindy. "I feel bad too. I wanted to protect it. But Tom, the alien could control you. Think of millions of those white worms, looking like tasty treats. People would eat them and then they'd be controlling people all over the world. They'd eat their food and make them do what the aliens wanted. It would be a disgusting, horrific nightmare!"

"You're right," said Tom.

Tom's dad came in, with Dr Wilson. Dad was very shaken up. He hugged Tom hard. Dr Wilson said Tom was lucky to be alive, and that he was a hero. He had defeated an invasion of evil, sneaky, food-sucking monsters.

"The aliens won't know where to find us now, and we'll be safe."

Tom was glad everyone was so pleased with him. But deep in his heart, he felt sad. He felt he was on his own again.

Chapter 11
Tom's Choice

Tom had to sign the Official Secrets Act. He swore he would never tell anyone what he knew. Lindy's dad went back to work with Dr Wilson, and Tom tried to forget all that had happened. He was only a kid. He would have to trust the grown-ups. He became good friends with Lindy. She wasn't an Alien Rights Activist any more, but she was still a little crazy and a lot of fun. He liked her a lot.

He worked hard to keep the weight off. He never ate too much, never touched sweet things and he took lots of exercise. He still loved food, but that was Tom's secret. He knew he must never give way to that love again.

One day when Tom cycled home from school he found a chocolate cheesecake standing on the kitchen counter. Mum's friends from work were coming to dinner and she'd made a special dessert. It looked incredibly tasty.

He went to his room so he wouldn't be tempted.

There was a terrible hole in his life that nothing would ever fill.

Perhaps in time he would forget, and food would mean nothing to him.

It was a sunny evening. He opened his window and looked out. Something small that had been perched on the ledge outside his room rolled in, and it fell to the floor. He bent down to see what it was, and there lay a sleek, delicious-looking chocolate bean.

Tom looked at the bean. The bean looked at Tom.

He thought he heard a faint voice in his mind.

I escaped, my friend. We can be together again!

Tom thought of the aliens on their far-away planet. Maybe they were starving to death right now. He thought of the white worm, and how Zock had taken over his body. What if the aliens were really evil? What if they came and destroyed the human race? Then he thought of that chocolate cheesecake, and all the other wonderful food he had loved so much. He remembered the warm feeling of having a friend inside.

He didn't know what to do.

Barrington Stoke would like to thank all its readers for commenting on the manuscript before publication and in particular:

Oliver Asher

Matthew Berry

Naomi Bourne

Oliver Butterworth

Joanna Douglas

Declan Gamble

Jane Griffiths

Peachs Hurlstone-Johnson

Charlotte Krikorian

Max Lawton

Sophie Lincoln

Annabelle Luce

Laura Malone

Lisa Marshall

Krishna Mistry

Thomas Newham

Holly O'Donnell

Jane O'Loughlin

Bridget Rogers

Jack Shenton

Anna-Kate Shingler

Become a Consultant!

Would you like to give us feedback on our titles before they are published? Contact us at the email address below – we'd love to hear from you!

info@barringtonstoke.co.uk
www.barringtonstoke.co.uk